For my Old MacMother, with love
—S.L.J.

To Captain Keith and Starboard Bob
—J.N.

BY
# Sally Lloyd-Jones

ILLUSTRATED BY
# Jill Newton

HARPER BLESSINGS
HarperCollins*Publishers*

# Old MacNoah Had an Ark

Old MacNoah built an ark, **Ee-i-ee-i-o**.
And for that ark he got some wood, **Ee-i-ee-i-o**.

With a **BANG! BANG!** here
And a **BANG! BANG!** there,
Here a **BANG!** There a **BANG!**
Everywhere a **BANG! BANG!**

Old MacNoah built an ark, **Ee-i-ee-i-o**.

And on that ark he had two cows, **Ee-i-ee-i-o**.

With a MOO! MOO! here

And a MOO! MOO! there,

Here a MOO! There a MOO!
Everywhere a MOO! MOO!

Old MacNoah had an ark,
**Ee-i-ee-i-o.**

And on that ark he had two ducks, **Ee-i-ee-i-o**.

With a
**QUACK! QUACK!**
here

And a
**QUACK! QUACK!**
there,

Here a **QUACK!** There a **QUACK!**
Everywhere a **QUACK! QUACK!**

Old MacNoah had an ark, **Ee-i-ee-i-o**.

And on that ark he had two pigs, **Ee-i-ee-i-o**.

With an OINK! OINK! here

And an OINK! OINK! there,

Here an OINK!

There an OINK!

Everywhere an OINK! OINK!

Old MacNoah had an ark,

Ee-i-ee-i-o.

And on that ark they had some rain, Ee-i-ee-i-o.

With a **SPLISH! SPLASH!** here
And a **SPLISH! SPLASH!** there,
Here a **SPLISH!** There a **SPLASH!**
Everywhere a **SPLISH! SPLASH!**

Old MacNoah had an ark, **Ee-i-ee-i-o.**

And on that ark they had some lunch, **Ee-i-ee-i-o.**

With a **BURP!
SLURP!** here

And a **BURP! SLURP!** there,

Here a **BURP!**

There a **SLURP!**

Everywhere a
**BURP! SLURP!**

Old MacNoah
had an ark,
**Ee-i-ee-i-o.**

And on that ark it got quite smelly, **Ee-i-ee-i-o**.

With a
POO! POO! here

And a
POO! POO! there,

Here a **POO!**

There a **POO!**

Everywhere a **POO! POO!**

Old MacNoah had an ark, **Ee-i-ee-i-o.**

And on that ark it got quite rough,

**Ee-i-ee-i-o.**

With an **OOPSIE-DAISY!** here

And an **OOPSIE-DAISY!** there,

Here an **OOPSIE!** There a **DAISY!**

Everywhere an **OOPSIE-DAISY!**

Old MacNoah had an ark, **Ee-i-ee-i-o**.

And from that ark they saw dry land,
**Ee-i-ee-i-o**.

With a **YA-HOO!** here
And a **YA-HOO!** there,
Here a **YA!** There a **HOO!**
Everywhere a **YA-HOO!**

Old MacNoah had an ark, **Ee-i-ee-i-o**.

And no more ark now, here's the end, **Ee-i-ee-i-o**.

With a
BANG! BANG!
here

...A SPLISH! SPLASH!
there

. . . Everywhere a

**BANG-SPLASH**

**OOPSY-MOO**

**QUACK-OINK**

**BURP-POO . . . YA-HOO!**

Old MacNoah had an ark,

Ee-i-ee-i-o!

HarperBlessings
HarperCollins Publishers
Old MacNoah Had an Ark
Text copyright © 2008 by Sally Lloyd-Jones   Illustrations copyright © 2008 by Jill Newton
Manufactured in China. All rights reserved.
For information address HarperCollins Children's Books, a division of HarperCollins Publishers,
1350 Avenue of the Americas, New York, NY 10019.   www.harpercollinschildrens.com

Library of Congress Cataloging-in-Publication Data
Lloyd-Jones, Sally.   Old MacNoah had an ark / by Sally Lloyd-Jones ; illustrated by Jill Newton.— 1st ed.       p.   cm.
Summary: After building his ark and loading it with animals, Old MacNoah must deal with mealtimes and their aftermath on the high seas.
ISBN-10: 0-06-055717-6 (trade bdg.) — ISBN-13: 978-0-06-055717-1 (trade bdg.)
ISBN-10: 0-06-055718-4 (lib. bdg.) — ISBN-13: 978-0-06-055718-8 (lib. bdg.)
[1. Animals—Fiction. 2. Boats and boating—Fiction. 3. Stories in rhyme.] I. Newton, Jill, 1964– ill. II. Title.
PZ8.3.J7538Old 2008   2006000342   [E]—dc22   CIP   AC

Typography by Carla Weise   1 2 3 4 5 6 7 8 9 10   ❖   First Edition